Freddie the Spider in the Snow

Ruth Emanuel

Dedicated to my Mum

Freddie woke up early one winter's morning and lay in his bed thinking to himself "what shall I do today?" It was very quiet, his mummy and daddy were still asleep, and the birds in the garden were just waking up and starting to sing. Freddie got out of bed and looked out of his bedroom window. "Oh my goodness!" he cried "mummy daddy wake up! the garden is covered by a white blanket!"

Freddie's mummy and daddy ran into his bedroom and joined him at the window "oh it's been snowing" said his mummy "how lovely and sparkly everything looks".

Freddie had never seen snow before and he couldn't wait to go and play in the garden. "You must have your breakfast first" said daddy "then you will have to put on your red wellington boots. The snow is cold and wet" "Okay" said Freddie "I'm so excited, I can't wait to play in the snow!" Freddie sat down at the kitchen table and ate a big bowl of porridge. "This will keep you nice and warm" said his mummy "you will need it if you are going out in the snow, its very cold".

So Freddie ate up all his porridge and after he had cleaned his teeth, he put on his red wellington boots, his coat, hat and gloves and once his mummy had made sure he was well wrapped up, Freddie opened the front door to go out. He couldn't believe his eyes! It looked even more beautiful than when he had seen it out of his bedroom window.

The whole garden was covered in white and sparkled like millions of stars. All the leaves on the trees had white hats on, so did the two bird tables. The chicken house roof was covered in snow and Freddie could see where the chickens had been walking in the garden; there were little chicken feet shapes in the snow. He took a step out of his house and his wellington boots sunk into the snow with a crunchy noise. The snow was fairly deep and Freddie had to walk carefully so that he didn't get stuck.

There was no one else in the garden; Freddie could see Mr & Mrs Brown, Gabriella and Jacob in the kitchen having their breakfast. So he walked carefully up the garden, making lots of little footprints with his wellington boots. He was having such a lot of fun! Then it happened! Freddie suddenly realised that he was standing right next to the dog kennel and he could see Rosie curled up inside. "Oh no" he thought "the snow makes the garden look different and Rosie's kennel is covered in snow so I didn't see it" Freddie turned to walk away but he lost his balance, slipped and fell head first into the snow. He was covered from head to foot in white and the snow had even got inside his wellington boots. Oh dear! But Freddie didn't mind! He picked himself up, shook all the snow off and walked quickly away leaving Rosie curled up in her kennel fast asleep. Whew! That was a narrow escape.

Then Freddie heard Jacob laughing and shouting. He was coming out to play in the snow and Freddie could see him pulling on his boots, putting on a coat, hat, scarf and gloves. Mrs Brown was telling him to be careful and to keep his hat and gloves on so that he didn't catch a cold. Freddie had reached the bird tables, he climbed up to the little table where he could sit and watch Jacob play.

Jacob ran out in to the garden and Freddie saw that he was with another boy. He was talking to the boy "come on Joshua, let's build a snowman" "Okay that sounds great fun! Is Gabrielle coming out too?" asked Joshua "No, she wants to stay indoors and play with her dolls" replied Jacob.

So the boys went running around the garden laughing and jumping in the snow. They made a little ball of snow which they then rolled around the garden until it became a very big ball of snow "I think that's enough for the body" cried Joshua "okay" said Jacob "let's put it here" They stopped rolling the big ball of snow and stood it in the middle of the garden quite near to the bird table where Freddie was hiding and watching them. "Right! Now we have to make the head" said Joshua.

Once again they started with a small ball of snow which they rolled around the garden until was big enough for the snowman's head. " That will do" cried Jacob "let's lift it onto the body" It was quite heavy and Freddie sat and laughed at the boys trying to lift the large ball of snow. It wasn't easy but eventually the boys managed to put the head onto the snowman's body.

"That looks good" said Mrs Brown, who had come to see what the boys were up to. "I think you will need a large carrot, some stones and a twig and a bobble hat. I will go and get the carrot and bobble hat. You two go and get stones and twig" "Thank you Mrs Brown" said Joshua "come on Jacob, let's start looking in the garden".

Freddie was a little confused as he was wondering why the boys needed a carrot, stones, twig and bobble hat. Can you guess why? See if you can before you carry on reading the story. Whilst the boys were looking around the garden, Mrs Brown came out of the house with a large carrot and woolly hat which had a big furry bobble on the top. "Here you are boys" she said "shall I fix the carrot for you?" "Yes please mummy" shouted Jacob and Freddie then watched Mrs Brown push the carrot into the middle of the snowman's face. Freddie now knew why a carrot was needed. Have you guessed? Yes that's right! it was to give the snowman a nose.

The boys then ran up to the snowman and laughed when they saw the bright orange carrot nose. They had collected a little twig and some stones and as Freddie watched from the safety of the bird table, he was once again a little confused, wondering what they were for. Do you know?

Jacob took two of the stones and put one stone on each side of the snowman's face above the carrot nose. Joshua then put the twig in the snowman's face under the carrot nose and that gave the snowman a mouth. It looked like the snowman was smiling! Freddie was so excited and laughed and clapped. The snowman had a lovely smiley face and when Jacob put the woolly hat with the furry bobble on top of the snowman's head, Freddie thought he looked just awesome!

Mr Brown then came out into the garden "Oh my! What a handsome snowman!" He said to the boys "all he needs now is some buttons to do up his coat and then he's finished. Give me four stones please Jacob". Jacob gave Mr Brown four stones and he put them in a line down the front of the snowman's body. Freddie thought that was very clever. The stones looked just like buttons on the snowman's coat. The snowman was finished and he looked terrific!

Mrs Brown then came out in the garden and called to the boys" come in now Jacob and Joshua. I have made you both hot chocolate as you must be cold". "Ooh yes please" the boys replied together and off they ran into the house.

Once the boys had gone, the garden was very quiet and Freddie decided it was safe for him to climb down from the bird table. He was feeling thirsty and hungry and knew he should be going home for his supper.

Freddie had really enjoyed his day in the snow and watching the boys build a snowman. He just loved being in the snow and hoped it would still be there tomorrow. He ran up to the snowman, looked up at him and said "Bye Bye Mr Snowman, I hope you enjoy your stay in our garden". Maybe I will see you again tomorrow" With that Freddie turned around and ran through the snow to his home at the bottom of the garden.

As it was near the end of the day, it was a lot colder in the garden and Freddie was looking forward to getting into his warm home. Maybe his mummy would make him hot chocolate to warm him up.

When he reached his home, just before he went in Freddie turned around and waved and smiled at the snowman. He was certain that the snowman smiled and winked at him. But maybe that was the snow twinkling and sparkling at him. What do you think??

Lightning Source UK Ltd.
Milton Keynes UK
UKHW050206031218
333179UK00002BA/5/P